Poems for Intelligent Children

With A Sense Of Humor

(This Means You)

Written by

Jack B. Jelinski

Illustrated by Adam Jelinski

www.buenasuertebooks.com

Library of Congress Cataloguing-in-Publication Data

Jelinski, Jack B. Poems For Intelligent Children

By Jack B. Jelinski

1. Children's Lit – Poetry. 2. Limericks. 3. Humor

ISBN # 0615893937

Book Design by Amy Sowers

Printed in the United States of America by **CreateSpace**.

Buena Suerte Books
433 N. Tracy Avenue
Bozeman, MT 59715

Dedication

For my grandchildren in order of appearance:

Maya, Sam and Olive

Acknowledgments

Thanks to my son Adam for sticking with this project as the illustrator of the book. To my wife Jane I am indebted for her forbearance during our great adventure of forty-four years. To granddaughter Maya, thanks for getting me invited to your school to play with poetry. To Brian Brandt and Louise Engelstad, thanks for counting syllables and the advice on age appropriate content. Finally, thanks to Amy Sowers, the 2011 National Champion boxer in the light flyweight division, for her assistance as the Book Designer.

To Purchase a Copy of This Book

visit www.buenasuertebooks.com

POEMS FOR INTELLIGENT CHILDREN

With A Sense Of Humor

(This Means You)

Jack B. Jelinski

Illustrated by Adam Jelinski

Buena Suerte Books | 433 N. Tracy | Bozeman, MT 59715 | www.buenasuertebooks.com

INTRODUCTION

Yes! I wrote these poems for you because I have always found children to be intelligent. All children. Some of the poems are very funny and short so you can learn your favorites and then recite them to your friends. Many of the poems teach lessons about how not to behave and others invite you to imagine things that are fun and crazy like dancing with a porcupine or teaching an emu to say cock-a-doodle-do. After you read some of these poems with your parents you can even write some yourself by just imitating some of the lines.

That's what happened when my granddaughter Maya's teacher, Mrs. Giovanelli, invited me to read my poems to her second grade class at Lakeridge Elementary School in Mercer Island, Washington. There were many "Kates" in the class, so we wrote this poem about Kate together:

There was a girl named Kate
Who everyone thought was great.
She was very smart
And had a great heart
But she could never get a date.

Some of the children wondered why Kate could never get a date if she was great and smart and had a good heart. That is the interesting part of writing poetry. Sometimes poems are written to make us think about things. I am sure you can imagine reasons why Kate might not get a date. After the class I thought it would be fun to change the poem and make it about a Praying Mantis:

There was a Praying Mantis named Kate.
All the boys thought she was great.
Even though she was nice
None dated her twice
'Cause she always bit the head off her date.

I am certain the Mercer Island Kate was not a Praying Mantis but it would explain why she could never get a date. I would not date a Praying Mantis. I think that many of these poems can be read before bedtime because they will make you feel calm and happy and even thoughtful. Others are about silly things kids think are funny like bad breath, poop and boogers. These are not for bedtime because they will make you laugh a lot. I hope you enjoy all of them!

Bad Manners
& Interesting Poems

It's A Crime

Sometimes it's a crime
when lots of words rhyme
like in this story of little Willy.
Believe me it's a dilly.
Willy was sometimes called Billy,
in his lapel he wore a lily
to school he rode a filly
because he lived where it was hilly.
When it got cold
he ate chili
and loved his aunt Tilli
who made him fresh piccalilli
which he ate willy-nilly.
Ok. I agree,
This whole poem is just silly!

Stinky Breath

My friend was a girl named McLeach.
Her breath smelled so bad I could screech!
Whatever I said,
she would never eat bread.
She just snacked on dead fish at the beach.

No Teef

A disobedient boy came to grief.
And what happened caused great disbelief.
Instead of brushing each day,
he'd just run out to play,
and then out fell all of his teef!

Liar, Liar

There are people who always lie.
Good liars are very sly.
Don't ever doubt
when they're found out
they just pretend to cry.

Dirk The Jerk

Please don't act like Dirk
who could bother, bedevil and irk.
He could even pester
his own ancestor
and always behaved like a jerk.

Amor In The Store

A woman who worked in a store
said, "Hola, mi amor."
I don't know why,
there was nothing to buy,
but I always went back for more.

Best Friend

Who is it you'll never offend?
On whom can you always depend?
Who you'd choose
to never lose
and be with until the end?

Dave in a Cave

There once was a boy named Dave
who didn't know how to behave.
He never acted nice
except once or twice
because he lived all alone in a cave.

Ruth and Billy

Sweet little Ruth
always told the truth
and had friends over every day.
Billy McBride
always lied
and was never invited to play.

Mean Gene

There was a boy named Gene
who always acted mean.
He was not really bad,
it just made him sad
that both of his parents were green.

Beans In His Ear

An odd, thin lad named Shameer
with eating habits most queer,
stuffed peas up his nose,
hid food in his clothes
and stuck green beans in his ear.

Stinky Kent

There's a stinky boy named Kent,
whose feet have a terrible scent.
Wherever he goes
people hold their nose
and it stinks wherever he went.

Long Hair

Becky "The Fair" had such long hair,
it reached all the way down to her toes.
I was pleased to see
when she looked at me
it didn't grow out of her nose.

Messy Rooms: Who Do You Blame?

Little Miss Bess
always made such a mess
and blamed it on naughty baboons.
When she fell asleep,
in they would creep
and spread toys all over her room!

Her sister Dixie
said that a pixie
threw her clothes on the floor at night.
But she told her mom
just to be calm
and she would make everything right.

Their friend Sally Delf
complained that an elf
with an innocent look on her face.
Would sometimes sneak in
then suddenly grin
and just toss stuff all over the place!

Now Molly McPeat
kept everything neat.
She put all her toys in a box.
An elf with a grin
couldn't get in
because her little box had locks.

Sweet Eve

A sweet little girl named Eve
caused her poor mother to grieve.
She kept her well dressed,
her blouses were pressed,
but she wiped her nose on her sleeve.

Don't Pick Your Nose

There was a girl who picked boogers named Jean.
Of nose-pickers she was the queen.
She stuck the best
up under her desk
and ate only the ones that were green.

A boy nose-picker named Rob,
would reach up and scrape a big gob.
He'd then roll it up
to store in his cup.
I thought it a very neat job.

Bob really loves picking his nose,
but never wipes boogers on clothes.
He puts them everywhere,
most often his hair,
where none of the icky stuff shows.

Of the many things you shouldn't do,
spitting is one, nose-picking is two.
Don't do it twice,
even once is not nice.
Kids will point and make fun of you.

Beer in Her Ear

Gena stuck things in her ear
and became unable to hear.
A doc checked her one day
and to his dismay
he pulled out a bottle of beer!

Fun
With
Kids
and Animals

The Brave Little Bird

She looked at the sky,
she needed to fly,
decided to do her best.
Didn't know if she could
she bravely stood
then jumped off the edge of her nest.

Ring Around the Skunk

Skunk played ring -'round the rosy,
we all played nice and cozy.
The skunk named Blinky
became quite stinky.
All who fell down held their nosey.

Frog Princess

A handsome prince out for a jog,
saw a princess asleep on a log.
His heart full of bliss,
he gave her a kiss.
She turned into a beautiful frog!

Bobbing For Apples With a 'Gator

Gail bobbed for apples with a gator.
We looked for her sometime later.
She didn't show up,
we asked 'gator, "What's up?"
"The apples were gone so I ate her."

The Lion's Feast

The mighty lion, king of beasts
invites everyone to his feasts.
But he's the only one
when feasting is done.
His guests are all soon deceased!

No Turkey For Thanksgiving

A turkey named Fred
never went to bed.
Exercised, getting thinner and thinner.
If he stayed thin
he knew he would win.
No one would eat him for dinner.

Ray Lost His Bray

A donkey named Ray
could no longer bray.
It made him feel like a ninney.
So he took a course
that was taught by a horse
so at least he could learn how to whinney.

Hey Doodle-Dow

Hey doodle-dow
I milked a brown cow.
She was as sweet as you could please.
I used milk from her udder
to make excellent butter
and some very good chocolatey cheese!

Don't Eat The Pig

There once was a pig
who danced up a jig
every time somebody would meet him.
He was very smart
and knew in his heart,
if he danced, nobody would eat him.

Emu

I tried to teach an emu
how to say cock-a-doodle-do.
But he just walked around,
and pecked at the ground,
then squawked loud and pooped on my shoe.

My Barking Dog

My dear dog Daisy
would bark like crazy.
Then she ran away, just departed.
It was just as well
because of the smell.
"cause each time she barked, she farted.

Froggy Doggy

If you had a dog
that croaked like a frog
and hopped on your walks in the park,
I would recommend
a frog for a friend.
You could look for a frog that could bark.

Dancing With Caroline

Dancing with Caroline
my friend the porcupine
led to an evening of thrills.
I was impressed,
with the way she dressed,
with a marshmallow on each of her quills!

My Mouse Boo

A mouse named Boo
loved to sleep in my shoe.
He was safe and had nothing to fear.
When he got older
he sat on my shoulder
and sang sweet, little songs in my ear.

Hey Doodle Do

Hey doodle-do,
a big kangaroo
hopped up and sat on my couch.
First we had tea,
and then she asked me
if I'd like to nap in her pouch.

Animals We Saw In Our Travels

In Italy, dogs ate scaloppini
and sometimes a nice fettuccine.
They'd bark and they'd bray
but just when they'd play
opera by Maestro Puccini.

In France we saw something rare.
A bear strolled right through the square.
Late in the day
he sat at a café,
read the paper, then ate an éclair.

In Florida we saw a Dalmatian
in a car getting gas at a station.
We asked her, "What's up
with you and your pup?"
And she said, "Oh, we're just on vacation."

After that we saw an Alsatian
playing Hearts with a friendly crustacean.
We approached with a grin
and asked, "Who will win?"
They said: "Silence, we need concentration!"

Then we saw something bizarre.
A chimp was driving a car!!
What was really weird ...
... he had a long beard,
and was smoking a Cuban cigar.

Zoo Is Out

A zoo keeper named McGee
let all the animals run free.
Every night at dark
lions roared in the park
and monkeys slept in our tree.

Maya Papaya

Little Miss Maya
ate only papaya.
The juice would drip down her chin.
Her little pup
would lap it all up
and she'd start all over again.

Wild
Imagination

Ears

There once was a boy named Wright
with ears so large he took flight.
Whenever a breeze
fluttered leaves on the trees
he could jump up and fly like a kite.

Mabel Under the Table

There was a young lady named Mabel
who chose to live under a table.
She frequently sends
invitations to friends
to visit whenever they're able.

Molly in Her Tree

Miss Molly McGee
she lived in a tree
where she loved to sip sarsaparilla.
At the end of the day
she would often play
cribbage with a friendly gorilla.

Tiny Tim Dreamed a Swim

Tiny Tim just loved to swim.
He dreamed a great swimmer he'd be.
He made a wish,
turned into a fish
and swam with the whales in the sea.

Where is Aaron Adair?

Our sweet friend Aaron Adair
one fine day went to the fair
and rode a machine that twirled.
He flew into the air
and came down who knows where?
We've looked all over the world.

Trick or Treat

In my trick-or-treat sack one Halloween
someone dropped in something green.
It looked like a worm,
and I could make it squirm,
but it tasted just like a bean.

The Lonely Fellow Named Jay

A lonely old fellow named Jay,
built his whole house out of clay.
He had friends in the house
and even a mouse.
All made out of papier-mache!

Backwards Pete

A backwards boy they call Pete
was the strangest guy you could meet.
No one understands
why he walks on his hands
and holds knife and fork with his feet.

Nose In The Wind

A big-nosed girl named McWound
is skinny, weighs scarcely a pound.
When a strong wind blows
it catches her nose
and spins her into the ground.

Hide-And-Seek

Marky McBride
sure knew how to hide
whenever we played hide-and-seek.
Once when we played,
so hidden he stayed
we didn't find him for a week!

Naughty Molly

We played hide-and-seek
with Molly McPeak.
We thought she got lost one night.
She went to the park
when it got dark
and gave us all quite a fright.
She did something bad,
didn't tell mom or dad
and went off to feed the deer.
We found her quite soon
by the light of the moon
glad we had nothing to fear.

Molly and Polly

Molly had a dolly
and called her Polly.
They wore the same clothes and shoes.
They were the same size
and both had blue eyes
so no one could tell who was who.

Jean Is Gone

Oh please, have you seen
our lost friend Jean?
She hid high in a tree one day.
We watched in surprise,
as before our eyes
a terodactyl snatched her away!

Fanciful Poems

and One Fairy

The Fairy Kiss

Once when I was in the deepest wood,
in the deepest wood one day,
I fell asleep among the flowers
when the fairies came out to play.

I awoke to the call of a cuckoo
perhaps the warbling of a wren.
The fairies cast a spell on me
so I can't remember when.

The first thing I saw was a butterfly,
so beautiful I could scarcely speak.
It fluttered down on a shaft of sun
and landed softly on my cheek.

Upon its back was a fairy,
an exquisite, gold creature was she.
She spoke in a voice sweet as nectar
and here's what she asked of me:

"You must write a poem about fairies,
then children will know I exist.
Proof I'll leave on your cheek tonight
that you were by a fairy kissed."

Then off she flew on her butterfly.
That's it, that's all she said.
I was released from the spell,
it was true, I could tell
because I awoke asleep in my bed.

So you must really believe in fairies
and in the truth of the story I've told,
for you can still see upon my cheek
a fairy kiss-freckle of gold.

You're invited to color the fairy!

Fairy Water
(Use Rose Water For This Recipe)

Fairy water's mixed with wild thyme,
clovers picked while ringing a chime,
buds of marigold
fresh, not too old,
stirred together while reciting this rhyme.

To enjoy a delightful surprise
touch the water to the lids of your eyes
with a gentle touch,
a drop, not too much
to see a fairy without her disguise!

The Fairies Request

The fairies told me other things
when I was under their spell.
I can't remember them all
but a few I remember well.

They shared the secret of fairy water,
wanted poems about the stars and the moon,
said I should add a leprechaun
so you could read this section soon.

The Moon

On a clear, dreamy night in June
a sweet girl sat watching the moon.
Her dad asked, "Can you see
if the moon's made of cheese?"
She took a small bite with her spoon.

Stars

Oh stars so bright,
so happy at night,
are you sad when you must leave the sky?
The morning dew
reminds me of you
'cause it sparkles like tears you might cry.

My Ears

I love my ears, I really do
I'm so pleased that I have two.
When I go to bed
both sides of my head
can hear you say "I love you."

My Nose

What's the point do you suppose
of my cute, amazing nose?
To sometimes get runny?
Get red and look funny?
Or smell the perfume of a rose?

Snow Angel

I made a snow angel one day.
To my great surprise
when I blinked my eyes
she got up and just flew away!

The Village Leprechaun

The village leprechaun was very old
and confused by his neighbors
if truth be told.
He tried to avoid it
but their kids used his toilet
'cause they thought he had a potty o' gold.

Monsters

Monster Croquet

I happen to know where monsters go
to hide out during the day.
Just as the sun rises,
they remove their disguises
and enjoy a nice game of croquet.

Bimble

I had a pet monster named Bimble
exceedingly tiny, but nimble.
One time, in our house,
he got chased by the mouse,
and hid out in my mother's thimble.

Grandpa's Monster

My grandpa kept his monster in the hall;
it was all rolled up in a ball.
When he got up at night
just imagine the sight.
Unrolled, he was eleven feet tall!

My Moose Monster

My monster Bruce
looked just like a moose
and always stood next to my bed.
Each night I chose
to hang my clothes
on a horn sticking out of his head.

The Canary Monster

The yellow monster wasn't scary
had feathers, wasn't hairy.
He'd sneak up on you
and try to shout boo!
but tweeted like a giant canary.

Good Monster Mark

A monster named Mark
would go to the park
and take care of girls and boys.
He'd hide out of sight,
and give a huge fright
to anyone stealing their toys!

Monster Pete's Feet

A monster named Pete
had more than two feet,
how many no one could say.
With more feet than a cow
no one knows how
he danced such a lovely ballet.

Our Garden Monster

Our monster Bunderdarden
protected our vegetable garden.
As the story goes
he scared all the crows
with his monstrous, awful fartin'.

Monsters Eat Lost Things

Before you're too old
you should all be told
that monsters don't eat real food.
For eating they choose
all the things we lose,
although it seems a bit rude.

Old Monster Larry

A monster named Larry
was no longer scary
and his nose was always red.
He had a bad cold
and had grown very old,
so I let him sleep under my bed.

Pretend

Pretend to fear monsters, please try.
Don't hurt their feelings, they're shy.
Don't laugh and be merry
when they try to be scary,
their hair gets all wet when they cry.

Dad or Mom Pretends To Be The Sleeping Monster

(A Game)

Your monster pretends to sleep on the floor,
closes his eyes and begins to snore.
This part's for you,
here's what you do:
sneak up and touch him before he can roar.

Sneak up and touch him, then run!
If he gets you first he's won.
If you get away
you've won the day
but try it again just for fun.

If you decide "Sleeping Monster" to play
remember he'll catch you one day.
He'll blow on your tummy,
you'll scream for your mummy
before you can get away.

The Bird Loving Monster

A big-haired monster named Ned
let little birds nest on his head.
The birds often chirped
and frequently burped
when he tossed up crumbs of fresh bread.

The End